Old, Older, Oldest

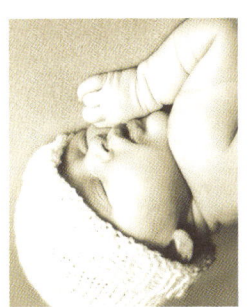

Written by
Stephen Rickard

This is Baby Sam.
Baby Sam is five days old.

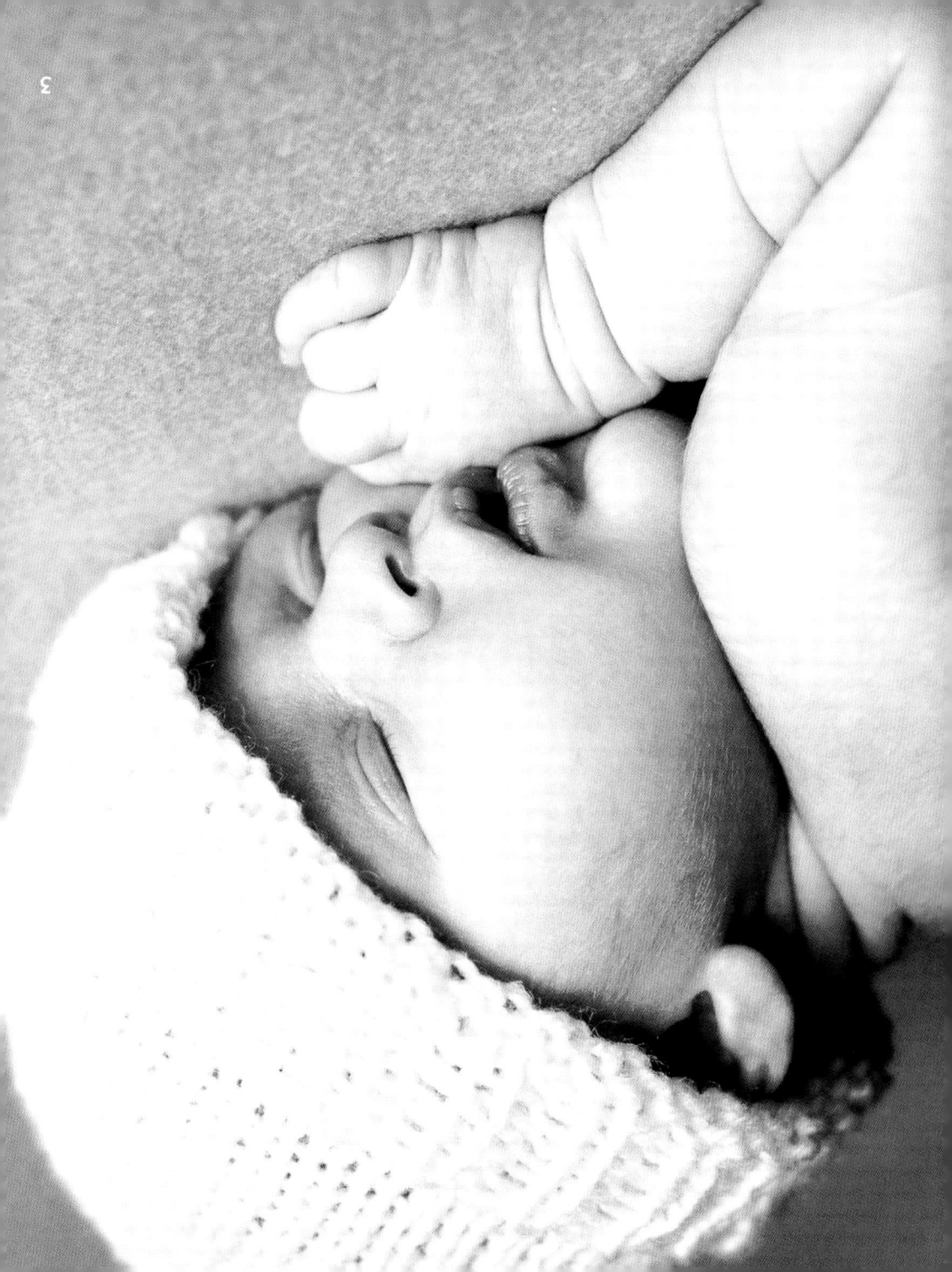

This is my brother.

My brother is six years old.

My brother is older than Baby Sam.

This is my mother.

My mother is thirty years old.

My mother is older than my brother and Baby Sam.

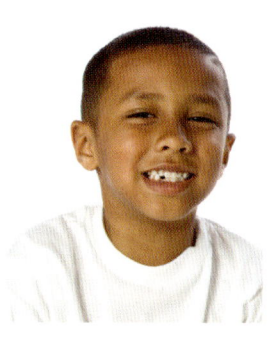

7

This is my grandad.

My grandad is sixty-two years old.

My grandad is older than my mother, my brother and Baby Sam.

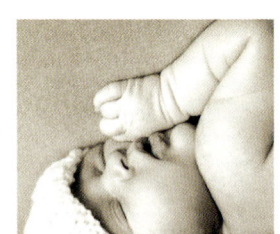

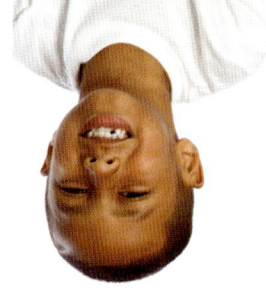  

This fish is 200 years old.

This fish is older than my grandad, my mother, my brother and Baby Sam.

11

This tree is 2,000 years old.

This tree is older than the fish, my grandad, my mother, my brother and Baby Sam.

 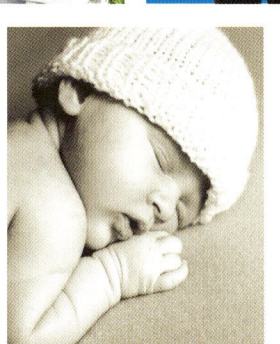

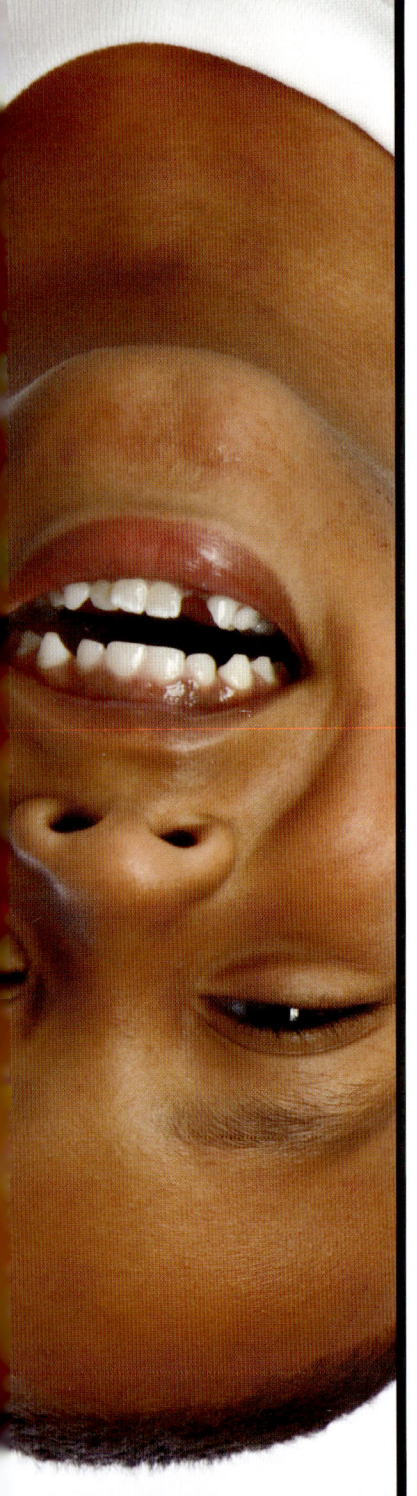

My brother and my mum are not old.
My grandad is older than my mum.
But he is not old.

The fish is old.
But the tree is the oldest of all!